First published 2005 by Walker Books Ltd
87 Vauxhall Walk, London SE11 5HJ

This edition published 2006

2 4 6 8 10 9 7 5 3 1

© 2005 Lucy Cousins
Illustrated in the style of Lucy Cousins by King Rollo Films Ltd

"Maisy" Audio Visual Series produced by King Rollo Films for Universal Pictures
International Visual Programming

Lucy Cousins font © 2005 Lucy Cousins

The author/illustrator has asserted her moral rights

Maisy™. Maisy is a registered trademark of Walker Books Ltd, London.

Printed in China

British Library Cataloguing in Publication Data:
a catalogue record for this book is
available from the British Library

ISBN-13: 978-0-7445-7089-2
ISBN-10: 0-7445-7089-1

www.walkerbooks.co.uk

# Maisy Goes
# to the Library

# Lucy Cousins

WALKER BOOKS
AND SUBSIDIARIES
LONDON • BOSTON • SYDNEY • AUCKLAND

Maisy likes going to the library.

How lovely to look at a book in a nice quiet place.

It was the sort of day when Maisy wanted a book about fish.

She found a flappy book about birds... but no fish.

She found a shiny green book about turtles...

and a great big stripy
book about tigers ...
but no fish!

Never mind,
there are
so many
other things
to do in
the library...

make a
copy of your
favourite
picture...

look at the
fish in the
aquarium...

# Aquarium?

That's it! So Maisy looked
by the aquarium...

and that's exactly where
she found a book about fish...
and it was sparkly!

Maisy settled down
to read in a quiet corner.

# But then Cyril and Tallulah came along...

and started laughing (at Tallulah's funny face!).

And then Eddie came in ...

because Ostrich was going to tell a story in the story corner...

Maisy's quiet corner!

# charley started laughing.

"She swallowed a dog to catch the cat!"

Then everyone started laughing!

And they were still laughing when they checked out their books,

# and went outside to play.

In the park, Cyril and Charley pretended to be the old woman and her dog.

Woof-woof!

Tallulah meowed like a cat...and
Eddie neighed like a horse.

Meeow!        And Maisy...?

Neigh!

Maisy read
her sparkly book
about fish in a
nice...quiet...
place...